THE ALIEN'S LOVE

GRACE KENSINGTON

1

ynx's mind was spinning. He didn't know what to think or how to react. He could hear the walls cracking and tearing as the massive creatures pulled themselves into the room, following each other so closely that they filled the doorway and crawled over one another grotesquely as if they couldn't wait to get to him. Lynx could only relate them to the spiders that Zuri had shown them pictures of while she was describing Earth and some of the types of life that lived there, but these were far beyond the small, scurrying bugs that she had shown them. Even the largest of those were miniscule compared to the gleaming creatures and their sharp, spiked legs that dug into the walls and ceiling as they crawled into the room.

As they moved toward him, Lynx stepped closer to the bed where Rain, the *human*, lay frozen in her calm, sleeping state. He had to protect her. He knew that this beautiful, delicate-looking woman, this lovely human that at once baffled and intrigued him, was meant to be his mate. It didn't matter to him that she was from a species that was not meant to have even visited Uoria before they started to arrive at the Denynso compound to research and learn, and even then were supposed to have been limited just to their area of the planet. It didn't even bother him that she had been lying here, frozen in her sleep, for longer than he had been alive. It was confounding and beyond his realm of comprehension, but at that moment the only thing that mattered to the warrior was making sure that the woman that lay in front of him was safe from these fearsome creatures crawling toward him.

There were seven of them now, leaving deep gouges in their wake as they moved across the walls and ceiling. He had seen gouges like that in the lower portion of the house when he had first arrived, but he had thought nothing of them. He had been far more concerned with the fact that in their desire to explore the planet of Uoria and discover what types of beings might share it with them, the group of Denynso men had found that there had been a long-running feud between two species that ended in one of them, the Covra, locking the beings they knew as the Light Ones, and that Lynx now knew were humans, in time, and that they were then roaming through that locked kingdom discovering everything that had stopped in the span of a breath, decades before.

Now what he worried about was Rain and how he would protect her. She couldn't move. As far as he knew, she had no awareness of what was going on around her. It was his responsibility to ensure that she was safe and that these creatures didn't harm her. He could continue to process the fact that she was human later. Right now he had to think quickly and get rid of these monsters.

Lynx stepped back toward the window that overlooked the street and could hear muffled screaming coming from the rest of the settlement. The creatures seemed to have found the rest of the Denynso men. Like the others, Lynx rarely carried weapons. They preferred to fight with their bare hands. And like the others, occasionally he carried a dagger that he had crafted himself. This dagger, however, he had left tucked in the bag he had been carrying as they walked from the compound, and he had dropped that bag to the floor near the door to the room.

He heard another scream from one of the buildings across the street and the frantic sound mobilized him. Lynx took a long stride across the room and dove toward his bag. He could feel something sharp grazing his back as he grabbed onto the bag and pulled it up against his chest. A fearsome hissing sound above him told him that he had angered the creatures, and he felt the sharp, piercing feeling in his back intensify.

Lynx reached into his bag and pulled out his dagger. In one fast movement he rolled over onto his back and slashed at one of the creatures. The tip of his dagger bit through the leg that was digging into his back and vibrantly green blood splattered down on him as the leg splintered off of the rest of the creature's body and skittered across the floor. The injured creature let out a horrific screeching sound and pulled back away from him, but even as Lynx saw the gleaming black thing withdrawing away from him, he watched as the open wound in the leg healed itself over and the limb started growing back.

Out of the corner of his eye Lynx saw one of the larger creatures climbing over the smaller one above his head, moving toward Rain where she lay on the bed. Lynx tightened his grip on the dagger and scurried backwards across the floor toward the edge of the bed. The large creature came toward him and he slashed at it with his dagger. Since he had watched the other creature heal itself so quickly, he didn't know how the larger one would react to his threats, but it was all he could do.

The creature took another step toward Rain and the fury built inside Lynx with an intensity that he had never experienced. He pulled himself up higher and changed his grip on his dagger so that it was pointing directly at the bulbous black eye at the front of the rounded body. He could see the reflection of his blade in the surface of the eye and as he leaned toward the creature, it stepped back. Lynx took another step forward and lay a protective hand on Rain's leg.

As soon as his hand touched her, Lynx felt his entire body tingle and saw a flash of bright, vibrant light. The room around him disappeared in the light and then reappeared, but it looked different. Sunlight, the type of dark, rich light that came with a late afternoon, made the room appear to glow. Out of the corner of his eye Lynx saw movement and he turned. Against the wall stood a vanity table with a large, curved mirror and at the table sat Rain.

2

———

Lynx started to reach toward Rain, and saw her look up into the mirror as if she could sense his presence. In the reflection in the mirror he could see just how beautiful she was, the sparkling blue of her eyes like nothing he had ever seen. As she looked into the glass, however, he realized that she wasn't looking at him, but something over her shoulder. He hadn't noticed anything, so he continued to watch.

Rain drew a brush through her long hair and then settled it onto the surface of the vanity table. She stood, the thin fabric of her nightgown skimming the curves of her body and brushing against the floor as she walked the few steps to the bed and slipped beneath the covers. Just as she settled her head onto the pillow and her body relaxed, he saw one of the massive black creatures climb out from under the bed. Lynx screamed, but it didn't do any good. The creature lifted one sharply pointed leg, the tip glinting even more gruesomely in the sunlight, and plunged it into Rain's stomach.

As suddenly and inexplicably as the vision had

appeared, the room around him seemed to melt and Lynx found himself standing back where he had been. It must have lasted only a few seconds, but Lynx felt like it had changed him completely. Something like that had never happened to him before. He wasn't even entirely sure what had happened, but those few moments had confirmed to him that these spider-like monsters were the Covra.

"Why?" he screamed at the one closest to him, and he saw it recoil as if it wasn't accustomed to hearing a spoken voice.

Lynx slashed at it with his dagger and the creature stepped backwards. He lunged forward and drove the tip of the blade toward the Covra's eye. It scurried backwards more quickly and Lynx rushed around the edge of the bed. The few moments of seeing Rain awake and vital had infuriated him to a level that was almost blinding, and he roared as he went after the Covra.

The louder he got, and the harder he slashed toward their eyes, the faster the creatures scurried toward the door.

"Lynx!"

Lynx heard Pyra's voice shouting up to him from the lower floor of the house. The deep sound of the lead warrior was encouraging. He knew that Pyra had survived and that he was not alone. A moment later Lynx heard Pyra's footsteps pounding up the stairs toward him, accompanied by another set. The horrific screeching of the Covra filled the space as Pyra and Bannack came into the room slashing at them with their own daggers. Green blood splattered the room and pieces of the creatures littered the floor.

"Their eyes!" Lynx shouted.

Pyra and Bannack turned their hands on the handles of their daggers, creating a tighter grip that allowed them to direct the carefully honed tips toward the rounded black domes of the Covra's eyes. The three warriors held their blades out toward the spider-like creatures, and for a moment they seemed to be retreating. As the room fell silent, however, the Covra's splintered limbs and the pieces of their round bodies that had fallen away under the edges of the Denynso's blades grew back and the monsters started to advance toward them again.

"Where are the other men?" Lynx demanded.

"They are fighting others of these creatures throughout the rest of the settlement," Pyra told him.

Lynx noticed that the Covra had stilled when they started speaking, and on instinct, he started again.

"These are the Covra," he told Pyra, pushing forward slightly with his blade held toward the eye of the closest creature.

"The Covra?" Pyra asked.

"Yes. The creatures that we read about in the prison in the compound. The ones that built the prison and locked this settlement."

"How could these things build a prison?" Pyra asked.

"I don't know, but they did, and now they are back here."

The men had managed to force the Covra back toward the door and they were scurrying away from them now, running along the walls and ceiling until they disappeared into other rooms and out of windows. Them being out of sight did not provide any relief for Lynx. He knew they were there, he knew now that they existed still and that they could appear out of seemingly nowhere. He didn't know how they had managed to make them retreat, and it was not comforting to him that he didn't know when they might return or how they could make them leave again.

The screams and hisses from outside had faded away as the Covra in the house disappeared and soon they were replaced by the shouts and frantic yells of the other Denynso. Pyra and Bannack started to run down the stairs toward the door to the house, but Lynx hesitated. He didn't want to leave Rain behind. Now that he knew that the Covra could return at any time, he felt like she was vulnerable. He rushed back into the room and knelt down beside the bed.

A moment later Pyra came back into the room.

"Lynx, come on. We have to find the other men. What are you doing?"

"I can't leave her," he said, gazing down at Rain.

"What do you mean you can't leave her?"

"This woman is supposed to be my mate."

He glanced up at Pyra and saw the look of confusion and shock cross his face. Finding their mate was something that the Denynso men waited for their entire lives. Unlike other species who may be able to mate with any number of others, the Denynso had one single mate. This was the only woman that existed in the entire universe who they could create a bond with, and the only one who they ever would create a bond with. They would look for that one woman throughout their entire lives, and when they found her, they immediately knew. After that, the bond was for life. This was something that they all knew from a very young age, and it took on even more serious meaning for Lynx now that he realized his mate was someone who may never again open her eyes.

"Lynx, this woman is locked in time. She has been here since long before you were even born, and she may be here on into eternity. You are just reacting to everything that's going on."

"No," Lynx said, feeling the defensive aggression building inside him, "Rain is my mate. She has been waiting for me for her entire life, and for mine."

"Rain?" Bannack asked, stepping into the room behind Pyra.

Lynx realized that the others didn't have any idea what he had discovered about these people, the Light Ones as the Covra had called them, and he debated with himself whether he should tell them. He worried that if he let them know that he knew they were human, they would not be as inclined to help them. Even though several of the Denynso, Pyra included, had mated with humans, there was still deep-seated controversy about how much interaction and connection the two species should have. The thought that they had been living on the planet all along, and that Creia had either not known about them or had been lying to them, could cause them even more difficulty than they were already facing.

Not telling them what he had seen, however, didn't seem like an option.

"I saw her," he said carefully.

"What do you mean?" Pyra asked.

"When the Covra were in here, I touched her, and I could see what I think were the last few seconds before she was locked."

"What did you see, Lynx?" Pyra demanded.

The force behind the words made Lynx feel even more defensive and he straightened his spine, pressing his chest toward the larger, older warrior. Suddenly Pyra's eyes widened.

"Lynx, you're bleeding," he said.

Lynx looked down and saw trails of his own blood sliding down his arm and dripping onto the floor beneath his feet.

3

___

"There's something wrong."

Elianna jumped up from the chair where she had been sitting and rushed across the room to Eden. She dropped down onto her knees next to her and rested her hands on the other woman's rounded belly.

"There's something wrong with the baby?" she asked frantically.

There was still so much that they didn't understand about Eden's pregnancy and every tiny twinge or moment of worry could bring panic to the other women. This was the first pregnancy for this generation of the Denynso, and even though Eden had technically become one of their kind when Ciyrs had saved her from near death, there was much of her that was still humanlike and no one knew how much of her pregnancy would resemble each of the species.

"No," Eden said, rubbing her belly as if to calm herself and the baby resting inside, "There's something wrong with Pyra."

Elianna's eyes widened and Eden could see the fear in them.

"What? What's happening?"

"I don't know," Eden said, straightening in her seat. "I can't communicate with him."

She concentrated hard on her mate, trying to make the connection that would allow them to speak to each other through their thoughts. It was a precious gift that the Denynso enjoyed with their mates, something that allowed them to connect in a way that was far deeper and more meaningful than the connection that they had with any of the others of their kind. She had learned, though, that this connection was not something that was always available. She couldn't just glance into Pyra's mind whenever she wanted to. If he was concentrating too hard on something else, or purposely did not want her to be able to see into his thoughts, she would not be able to. She knew the same went for her, but she rarely closed him out. The fact that she could sense that there was something wrong with him but was unable to decipher exactly what it was, or to communicate with him, frightened her.

"Try Ciyrs," Elianna said.

Eden looked into her friend's eyes. She could see the lingering pain there that the small woman always tried to conceal, but occasionally made itself sharp and inescapably known.

"You can't get to him?" Eden asked.

Elianna shook her head.

"Try him, please."

This was another of the extraordinary things about Eden that made her stand apart from the other mates of the Denynso despite them all being quite close. She was not only the first of the human women to come to the planet and find her mate in one of the tremendous warriors who guarded the compound and waged war against other species throughout the galaxy. She was the first to find herself pregnant with the child of one of the warriors. And she was the only human that the Denynso healer Ciyrs had brought back from the brink of death after a gruesome encounter with one of the Klimnu. It was during that inter-action that she had been turned into one of them, and in turn she had formed a link with Ciyrs that was just like the one she had with Pyra.

It was the only such link that existed in the Denynso. Usually only the men and their mates formed the link that allowed them to speak through their thoughts and feel each other's emotions. Eden and the healer, however, had created that link and still maintained it. Their bond was nothing like hers with Pyra, or his with Elianna. It was not romantic, but rather she saw him as her most treasured friend, like a brother that she had never had during her time on Earth. The link had extended to her and Elianna, but they rarely used it. The fact that she and Ciyrs were connected in such as way was already difficult for their mates, even though both Pyra and Elianna had expressed time and time again that they understood that they didn't represent a threat to their bonds. Out of respect for their mates, however, Eden and Ciyrs agreed to stay away from each other's thoughts as much as possible, only entering them in times of emergency.

Ciyrs?

Eden sent out the call to Ciyrs, barely breathing as she waited for him to respond.

Please, Ciyrs, talk to me. Elianna says that she can't get to you, and I can't get to Pyra. I know that there's something wrong. Talk to me.

She got no response and the fear that had been building inside her sharpened to an almost painful edge. She hadn't wanted Pyra and the other men to go out into the rest of the planet to explore. The battles with the Klimnu were still so fresh and raw in their minds, and the death of Jem was still so painful. The thought of them leaving the compound, venturing outside of the boundaries for the first time of any of their kind, was terrifying to her, especially as she moved further along in her pregnancy. She was so scared that something was going to happen to them and that she would be without Pyra, a thought that made her feel empty and hollow inside. She had left everything that she had ever known on Earth to stay on Uoria to be with him, something that she would do again in a second if she had to make the choice, but the thought of losing him was far more difficult and painful than walking away from anything she had known in her life before him.

"They've only been gone a day," Eden said, trying both to convince herself and Elianna that everything was fine, "What possibly could have happened to them? They are probably just sleeping."

Even as the words came out of her mouth, though, she knew that she didn't believe them. She had reached out to both Pyra and Ciyrs when they were sleeping before and they had woken up immediately. She had learned to enter their thoughts carefully enough that she would be able to tell if they were dreaming, something she did with tremendous caution after some of the dreams that she had stumbled into when connecting with Ciyrs, and she knew that as forcefully as she had just tried to connect with both men, they would have woken up.

"Where are the others?" Elianna asked, "Maybe they can get to their mates."

"Zuri said that she, Leia, and Samira would be down by the water. They've decided to do more of their research while the men are gone."

"They aren't going back to Earth, are they?"

"Not for any longer than Samira and Ty's wedding," Eden paused, not wanting to say out loud what the worrisome little voice in the back of her mind was saying, questioning whether that wedding would ever actually come to pass. "But I think that it distracts them. Their whole lives on Earth were the university and their teaching or studies. Maybe it helps them not think about their mates."

The two women had started out of the house toward the water and Eden could feel Elianna staring at her as they walked.

"Do you ever miss your work?" Elianna asked.

Her voice was low, as if she was trying to keep what she had said just between her and Eden, though the compound was nearly deserted now that the men were gone. The human mates still had little to no contact with the Denynso women, except for the midwives, and for the most part the five of them existed on their own.

"No," Eden said honestly, "That job, as proud as I was of it, was awful. My boss was... horrible."

She realized as she said this that she had never really told the other women how she had made her way into the Denynso compound. As the first to become a part of the clan, she had watched the other women join them one by one, but she hadn't really opened up to them about her experiences before she made the decision to stay with Pyra.

"What happened?" Elianna asked.

Eden sighed. She had wanted to leave her past behind her, to keep it firmly on Earth so that she didn't have to deal with it any longer, but she knew that it wouldn't help her to pretend like none of it had ever happened.

"My boss, Ryan, was not a nice person. He wanted what he wanted and he was going to get it, or make everybody's life miserable. I wouldn't date him, so he decided to send me on what he thought was a death mission."

"What?" Elianna sounded horrified.

"Yeah. A bit of an overreaction if you ask me, but that's what he decided to do. He knew that the Denynso had very strict rules about human visitors, particularly scientists, and he sent me here with the specific instructions to go against those rules."

"What did he want you to do?"

"He wanted me to bring back a sample of Denynso warrior blood so that he could analyze it and find out what makes them so powerful. Of course, that is the most serious rule that the Denynso have. To Ryan, either I would be successful and he would be able to get to the source of the Denynso power and possibly create his own race of superior warriors through genetic engineering on Earth, or I would get caught and they would kill me. Either way, he would get something that he wanted; success and fame, or revenge."

"Where is he now?" Elianna asked.

Eden glanced over at her. She honestly hadn't thought about him in the months that she had spent on Uoria. It was as if he didn't exist anymore.

"You know, I have no idea. It's possible that the research lab thinks that I'm dead and they've brought him up on endangerment and espionage charges."

The thought delighted Eden on a level that she didn't necessarily want to admit to anyone, and it made her feel a little less awful about herself when Elianna laughed.

"That would serve him right," she said.

Eden laughed.

"It would. I'm sure that he would absolutely love a few decades in one of the prison tech camps."

The thought of Ryan chained to one of the expansive computers in the technology prison camps, forced to work from morning until night working systems so basic they would drive him mad, was enough to assuage all of the anger she had for him, and she found herself smiling as they walked on toward the pond at the far end of the compound.

Her smile faded, however, when she saw Loralia running toward them, her long braid bouncing on her back as she rushed down the dirt road, her compact held tightly in her hand. Suddenly Eden remembered why they were walking toward the water and all of the fear and heartache came rushing back.

4

Pyra held Lynx down on the floor, pushing his arms down against the wood with nearly all of his strength. Even though the younger warrior was smaller, the ferocity that was suddenly pouring out of him was making it more difficult than Pyra would have imagined for him to control his thrashing. As soon as he had mentioned the blood dripping from Lynx's back, the other warrior had seemed to snap, suddenly becoming aggressive and violent toward him and Bannack. He was hissing in a way that was almost like the Covra, and no matter how loudly Pyra shouted his name, he stared back at him through eyes that looked dark and unrecognizable, as if they were not registering the meaning of the word.

Behind him Bannack gripped a silver compact in his hand and stared into it. The compact looked like a larger, heavier version of the one that Loralia carried and Pyra wondered what Bannack could possibly be doing with it as he struggled to not only fight off Lynx's violent reaction, but to understand what was causing it.

"Loralia!" Bannack suddenly gasped.

"Bannack?" Loralia's voice came into the room and Pyra shot a shocked look at Bannack, "What's wrong?"

"Something's happening to Lynx," Bannack said into the compact, "We don't know what's going on."

"What happened?"

"I can't get into the whole story right now, but he's been injured and now he seems like he's completely out of his mind. He's fighting Pyra and we can't get him to calm down. He looks like he's trying to kill him."

"Show him to me."

Pyra forced his knee into Lynx's chest to give him more control over him and watched as Bannack came closer and held the compact at an angle as if reflecting Lynx in the mirror.

"What are you doing?" Pyra asked.

"If anyone would be able to figure out what's going on with him, it's going to be Loralia."

"How was he injured?" Loralia asked through the compact.

Her voice sounded slightly strained, as if she knew something but didn't want to actually say it until she knew for sure that she was right.

"We encountered another species..."

"The Covra," Loralia said before Bannack could even continue his sentence.

"Yes," Bannack said, "You've heard of them?"

"Yes. A long time ago. I didn't know that they still existed. You need to get Lynx to Ciyrs as fast as you possibly can."

"What's wrong with him?"

"He's been infected by the Covra. They are fairly weak creatures. They have their talons, but their greatest form of defense is infecting those they are fighting. If they can get their venom into another creature, that creature forgets what it is and tries to kill anything near it. The effect lasts until the venom is removed, or the infected creature is destroyed."

"I don't understand. If they can turn whatever they get near into killing machines, how are they weak? Why aren't they able to just destroy whatever comes their way?"

"They used to, and then other species realized that it takes many, many years for them to reproduce, and that they have a very specific vulnerability. They were once feared more than anything on this planet, but several generations ago they came in contact with an enemy that took that power from them. They found that vulnerability and were able to stave them off."

"The Light Ones," Bannack said.

"I don't know," Loralia admitted, "I only know what my grandfather told me. He said that their numbers were greatly diminished and that they had to wait for the next generation to be born before they would be able to fight again. They haven't been heard from since."

"You don't know what their vulnerability is?"

"No, but you need to get Lynx help now. The longer you wait, the harder it will be for Ciyrs to remove the venom. If you wait too long, Lynx will kill until he is killed."

"Thank you," Bannack said, "I love you."

Pyra watched him snap the compact closed and look down at him. His arm muscles were starting to burn from forcing Lynx to stay in place on the floor and he was pushing down into his chest with his knee so hard that he worried he was going to break his ribs.

"How are we going to get him to Ciyrs?" Pyra asked, "If I let up even a little, he's going to get off this floor and that dagger is far too close to him for my comfort if Loralia is right about him being infected."

"You're going to have to hold him while I go find Ciyrs. Where did you last see him?"

"He went into a building down the street. I don't know where he is now."

Bannack looped the braid of Loralia's hair that held the compact back over his neck and ran out of the room. Pyra listened to his footsteps pounding down the stairs and fade as they left the house. He could only hope that he was able to find the healer in time to save Lynx. He didn't want them to lose one of their men on the first day of a trip that he was supposed to be leading.

THE BLOOD WAS RUSHING through his veins so hard that Bannack could hear it in his ears as he ran out of the house and back out onto the dusty street. He could hear the voices of the other men coming from the buildings and down the street, and he struggled to decipher Ciyrs's among them. He had heard the guilt and worry in Pyra's voice, but he felt like he was the one that should feel guilty. It was him that had first pointed out that the Denynso knew almost nothing about the planet that their kind had always called home, and that by never leaving their compound they had made it so that none of them knew what types of creatures might exist beyond it. It had been him that had first suggested that they should go out and explore. Pyra might feel like as the leader of the Denynso warriors, it was his fault if anything went wrong, but Bannack knew that if he didn't find Ciyrs in time, he was responsible for whatever horrors followed with Lynx.

Bannack saw Ty coming down the street toward him and Bannack ran for him, reaching out and grabbing the other man's shoulders as soon as he was close enough.

"Have you seen Ciyrs?" he demanded.

"What?" Ty asked, "What's wrong?"

"Have you seen Ciyrs?" Bannack asked again, staring intensely into the baker's eyes. "Lynx is injured and needs him now."

Worry rolled over Ty's eyes and he shook his head.

"I haven't seen him."

Bannack let go of him and continued down the street. Around him he saw the other warriors streaming out of the buildings and coming onto the street from other areas of the settlement. Many of them had the vibrant green blood of the Covra streaked across their skin or soaked into their clothing. They all had confused, horrified expressions on their faces that told him that they were just as stunned by what had just happened as he was.

"What the hell were those things?" someone asked from one side.

"Did you see their legs grow back?" another voice asked.

"Where did they go?"

Bannack continued to run down the street, his heart pounding so hard that he could feel it in his throat and he felt like he was going to get sick. This isn't what he had in mind when he suggested that they go out onto Uoria and discover what was waiting outside their compound walls. When he first mentioned it, it was motivated by his painful emotional response to Jem's death and the fear that came from the fact that he died in a place that none of them even knew existed. When he went to Pyra and told him that he wanted to go with them, it wasn't truly out of a deep need to understand what was on the rest of the planet, but out of fear of his feelings for Loralia and his desire to escape from her. Through his haste and selfishness he had put the warriors in more danger than they had ever been in.

With their other enemies, they had known what they were facing. They knew what the creatures were and how they could defeat them. Right up until they were in the mirror realm coming up against the Klimnu for the final time, they were always on their home ground, comfortable and secure in knowing where they were and the resources that they could use to fight. Now they were somewhere they had never been, surrounded by unfamiliar landscape and facing enemies that they didn't know and didn't understand. The Covra were gone for then, but they could show back up at any moment, and without even knowing what their vulnerabilities were, the Denynso had little chance of defeating them.

5
____

Loralia looked at each of the women, gauging their reactions to the conversation she had just had with Bannack. As soon as he had begun to contact her, she had sought out the other women, feeling that if something had gone wrong on the quest with one of their mates, they deserved to know as soon as she found out. She was beginning to know and trust these women, and she didn't want to do anything that might hurt them in any way, or cause them to distrust her as the others had when they first encountered her, and that included keeping anything that she knew about the men or their quest from them for even a moment.

Eden looked back at her with one hand over her mouth, the other cupped around the front of her belly in the protective stance that she assumed most of the time. Zuri looked dumbstruck, looking up at them from where she knelt by the side of the water just as she had been when Loralia, Eden, and Elianna rushed up to her after Loralia found the other two women nearly at the pond. Elianna was trembling, one hand gripping Leia's hand beside her as if seeking out the support of the tiny woman.

None of them said anything for several long seconds. Loralia didn't push them and she avoided reflecting their feelings, not wanting to delve into the private moments that each of them were having. She didn't know what they were thinking or what they were feeling, but she was quickly learning that the human women were not as open to having their emotions explored as her kind was. She was trying to learn to rely not on her ability to decipher the feelings and emotions of those she encountered, but rather their words and actions when she wanted to interact with them.

"Be honest with us, Loralia," Leia said carefully, "How much danger are they actually in?"

Loralia wasn't sure how she was supposed to respond to that question. The truth was that she had told Bannack everything that she knew about the Covra. The fearsome creatures were something that the older ones of her kind had told stories about when she was younger. Her grandfather was known for weaving elaborate tales in the tradition of Loralia's kind, meant to both frighten the young ones in the delightful way that they enjoyed, and to teach them about the history of the planet. Many of these stories had long since left Loralia's memory, but the ones about the Covra had always lingered with her. Something about creatures that were so different from them and fought in such a vicious manner had deeply bothered Loralia, and she had never forgotten what her grandfather had said about them.

"I wish that there was more that I could tell you," she said, "but what you heard me tell Bannack is everything that I know about the Covra. I don't know what species they encountered that finally found their vulnerability, or what that vulnerability may be. All I know is that Ciyrs doesn't have a lot of time to get the venom out of Lynx before it will be too late."

"Will he kill Pyra if he gets away from him?" Eden asked.

Her voice was low and soft, but controlled. It was the voice of a woman fighting to maintain her composure, refusing to allow herself to give into the emotions that were threatening her so that she was as calm and even as possible to ensure she didn't miss any critical information about the mate for whom she lived and breathed. Loralia wanted to comfort her, but she couldn't lie to her.

"Yes," she replied.

Eden looked like she had been struck. She stepped back slightly, shaking her head as if she could make the situation go away by denying what Loralia had just told her.

"Ciyrs will get to him," Elianna said confidently, "He will. And he will get the venom out and heal him. He is the best healer that has ever been, and he brought all of his ointments and supplies with him. There is nothing that they could encounter that Ciyrs would not be able to heal."

Loralia nodded, allowing Elianna's words to comfort her. She longed for the ability to communicate with Bannack through her mind the way that the other women could communicate with their mates. Though they had not been able to connect with them that day, they knew that at some point soon they would be able to reach out with their minds and feel what their mates were feeling, know what they were thinking, and send their own thoughts to them. She only had her compact and the shared link that it created with Bannack. Though she was incredibly grateful for that, it was one of the things that made her feel separated from the other women. They had been truly welcoming to her since she had made the decision to join the compound with Bannack, but Loralia still felt like they existed in two entities; the five of them and her. Though they were getting closer and the human women were doing what they could to make her feel like a true part of the clan, there was still enough space between them that Loralia felt like she was looking into their experiences rather than truly being a part of them.

"Is there anything we can do?" Zuri asked, standing up and brushing the dirt off of her knees.

"All that we can do is wait to hear from them again and hope that the next time that we do it will be with good news about Lynx," Loralia said.

Eden shook her head.

"No. That's not enough. I can't just sit around and hope that Ciyrs gets to Lynx and gets the venom out of him before he tires Pyra out and kills him."

"What do you want to do?" Leia asked.

"We have to go talk to Creia. He might not know much about the rest of Uoria, but he knows more than the rest of the Denynso, and far more than us. Maybe if we tell him what the men told us and what Loralia knows, he will be able to tell us more and we can piece it all together."

There was a moment of unspoken agreement amongst the women and they all started toward the meeting hall together, hoping that when they arrived the king would be able to tell them something that could ease their fears and help them to feel more comfortable with the men being gone for longer.

They expected that Creia and his queen Theia would be in either their sitting room where they held formal meetings or in their living quarters when they arrived, but when the women got to the meeting hall fifteen minutes later, they found the king and queen standing on the front steps as if waiting for them.

"Oh! Hello, ladies," Creia said happily, holding out his hands in greeting, "I just sent Zsilvia to find you."

"Is everything alright, sir?" Zuri asked.

"Of course!" Creia said, "I just wanted to make sure that you are ready for the arrival of the new teacher."

Loralia glanced over at the other women and saw them all exchanging quizzical looks.

"New teacher?" Zuri asked.

Loralia had learned a little about the university exchange program that had brought Zuri, Elianna, Samira, and Leia to Uoria, and she had assumed that even though the women had decided to make the planet their home rather than returning to Earth at the end of what had been intended to be a few months' stay, that the program would continue. From the way that the human women were reacting, however, it didn't seem that they knew anything about this new teacher.

"I didn't know that the university was sending any other teachers," Samira said, looking at Zuri, who shook her head as she continued to stare at Creia.

"Neither did I. The plan was that I would be the first professor to come and then when I returned and shared my research with the rest of the university, we would plan for more teachers to come here and students from the compound to go to Earth."

"We received communication from the university a couple of weeks ago saying that they were sending another professor to join you," Creia said. "I told you about it that day."

His voice had lost some of the jovial happiness that it had had as they approached and Loralia felt herself fall back into her protective default of reflecting the emotions of the king so that she could prepare herself for what may be happening. The man felt frustrated, but also slightly confused, as if he wasn't entirely sure about what he was saying. He seemed to be thinking through the situation, going back through the memory that he thought he had of telling Zuri about the impending arrival of the new professor, and finally settling on disappointment.

"I'm sorry," Zuri said, "I really don't remember."

"Zuri, of all people I would think you understand the importance of this program to Uoria and to the Denynso. I know that your path changed when you came here and you have decided to stay with us, and of course we are all delighted that you have found your home and your mate among our people, but that means that in order for the program to continue and our hopes of cooperation with the humans of Earth to come to reality, we have to have another professor come."

Beside Loralia, Zuri felt stung and embarrassed. Loralia looked at her and saw the blonde woman nodding, her pale cheeks suddenly aflame with color.

"Of course," she said in a voice that sounded somewhat defeated.

"Good. Please do what you need to do to ensure there is a cabin prepared for the shuttle arrival. With the men gone, I am having Zsilvia act as escort and guide, so if possible find a home that is close to hers."

The king turned away and went back into the meeting hall, leaving the women looking up at Theia.

"You will have to forgive my mate," she said soothingly, "He feels anxious with the warriors gone. He wants you to make sure everything is ready because he trusts you. He trusts you more than he does any of the Denynso women, and that is saying a lot."

She said this with a type of conspiratorial note in her voice that made the five human women more at ease, but Loralia could still feel a sense of guarded worry coming off of Zuri.

"I really don't remember him mentioning another professor to me," Zuri said.

"To be honest, Zuri," Theia said, "He might not have. With all of the chaos that has been going on around here, he might have only thought that he mentioned it to you because he intended to. If it helps at all, I was there when he communicated with the university and they said that this professor is very excited to join you and be a part of the program."

The Denynso queen smiled kindly at the women and then turned to join her mate in the meeting hall. Zuri turned to the other women, shaking her head.

"I really don't remember anything about this new professor," she said.

"Neither do I," Samira agreed.

"Is that a problem?" Loralia asked, venturing to join the conversation that she had been trying to follow but didn't quite understand.

"We found out that a human flight attendant who had been on every shuttle from Earth had been helping the Klimnu and was instrumental in them being able to take over your mirror realm. If it hadn't been for her, none of us would have gone through the things that we did at the hands of the Klimnu. The only one of us who they didn't attack is Samira, and that's only because she came here just before the final battle. If they had had the opportunity, they would have tried to get her, too. It makes it very difficult for us to trust."

She hadn't meant to, but Loralia felt herself take a step

back from the rest of the women. Eden held up a hand as if to stop her.

"She didn't mean..." she started.

Loralia shook her head.

"No, it's alright. After everything that all of you have gone through, I don't expect you to trust me immediately."

She turned to walk away from them, wanting to be back in the little house that she shared with Bannack, when she heard Zuri's voice again.

"We really are happy to have you here, Loralia. I hope you know that."

Loralia nodded, but continued on her way back home.

6

Bannack was nearly at the end of the main street of the locked settlement when the door to a building beside him opened and Ciyrs stepped out. He was so relieved that for a moment he wasn't even able to move, but when the healer started in the opposite direction, Bannack reached out and grabbed ahold of his shirt.

"Come on," he said, starting to pull him down the street back toward the house where Pyra and Lynx were.

"What's wrong?" Ciyrs asked.

"Lynx has been injured. We need to get there as fast as we can. I'll explain on the way."

Apparently understanding the urgency of the situation, Ciyrs started running beside Bannack, weaving in and out of the other warriors and the people locked in time as they made their way back down the street. Many of them shouted after them, but they didn't pause. As they ran, Bannack explained as concisely as he could what had happened to Lynx and what Loralia had told them about the venom. He was relieved that the healer had his bag still strapped across him and was already digging through its contents by the time they reached the front door to the house.

Bannack could hear Pyra and Lynx still struggling on the floor above them and despite the ferocity of the sounds, he was relieved because it meant that the huge lead warrior had managed to maintain control over Lynx and the infected man had not broken free and killed him. As long as they could hear the grunting and thrashing, he knew that they still had time.

They climbed the stairs two at a time, and when they entered the bedroom, Ciyrs dropped his bag to the floor. He held a strange-looking contraption in one hand.

"Where was he injured?" he asked.

Pyra's eyes snapped up to him as if he hadn't even noticed that the other men had come into the room.

"His back. I don't know how bad it is."

"Bannack says that it took several minutes for the reaction to start."

Pyra let out a loud grunt and forced Lynx back down onto the ground. By now both men had bloody gashes in their arms and Pyra had blood streaming down his face from where Lynx had apparently reared up and broken his nose.

"Yes. He didn't start acting like this until the Covra were already gone and I pointed out that he was bleeding."

"Hopefully that means that they didn't get too much venom in him and that I'll be able to get it out easily."

"Have you ever heard of this before?" Bannack asked from the doorway.

"No, but I've dealt with other venomous creatures. I'll do the best I can. Pyra, when you feel like you have enough control, flip him over onto his belly. Bannack, come around the side and as soon as he's over, grab onto one of his arms and help Pyra hold him. This is going to be painful, so make sure you are holding him down hard enough and expect some screaming."

He said it all with such calmness that Bannack almost thought that Ciyrs was joking, but when he looked at him, he could see the intensity in the healer's eyes and he knew that he was absolutely serious. Bannack hurried around to Lynx's other side, poised to help Pyra hold him down. A moment later Pyra released the hold that he had on Lynx with his knee in his chest and let go of one of his arms so that he could flip the man over onto his belly. Lynx thrashed, nearly forcing Pyra back, but Bannack grabbed hold of him and together they were able to fight him back to the ground.

They held him in place long enough for Ciyrs to press the contraption to the long gash down Lynx's back and start turning the handle at the top. Lynx let out a primal scream and his entire body tensed. Ciyrs turned the handle faster, seeming to intensify the drawing of the venom the more the warrior responded. Finally Lynx's body relaxed and he seemed to collapse onto the floor. Bannack could see his eyelids fluttering over his closed eyes and hear his labored breath, but his body didn't move even as he and Pyra started to ease their grip on him.

"You can let go," Ciyrs told them, seeming to notice how cautiously and reluctantly the two men were releasing their hold on Lynx, "He's going to be asleep for a good while. I'm going to have to heal him up now, and all of that takes a lot out of you." Ciyrs gestured for his bag and Pyra handed it to him, "Where do you want me to take him? He's going to have to have somewhere to lie down."

Bannack watched as Ciyrs started pulling bandages and

healing ointments out of his bag and setting them on the floor beside Lynx's prone figure.

"Here," Pyra finally said.

Bannack and Ciyrs both look up at him sharply.

"Here?" Ciyrs asked, "Why?"

Pyra gestured at the bed against the wall, the one with the woman that Bannack had completely forgotten even existed. It looked even stranger now to see her lying there, not reacting in any way to everything that had just happened around her.

"He says that she is his mate."

"But she's..."Ciyrs started to protest and Pyra held up a hand to stop him.

"I'm well aware," Pyra said, his voice sounding tired as if the fight with Lynx had taken everything out of him physically and emotionally, "but it is none of my business who he thinks is his mate. We all know what it's like when we first found our mate. It might not have been the easiest thing in the world, and it might not have made terribly much sense at the time, but we knew. Even those of us who tried to deny it," he shot a glare at Bannack, who tried to pretend he didn't see it, "and if being with Eden and watching all of you find your mates has taught me anything, it is that we never know what's going to happen. If he thinks that this woman is supposed to be his mate, I think that he should be here with her. If nothing else, make him more comfortable so he heals better."

Bannack and Ciyrs nodded, and Bannack could only imagine that the healer was thinking back, just as he was, about when he found his own mate. It wasn't an easy process, and one that changed his life from the very first moment that it started. As hard as he had tried to deny his immediate and intense love for Loralia from the first time that he saw her, he had felt the changes that came over him even before he had laid eyes on her. The intensity, aggression, and anger that had coursed through him had been like nothing he had ever experienced, and though he was able to explain those feelings away as being a part of his reaction to the impending battle, he had not been able to give the same explanation to the overwhelming arousal that had come over him as he approached the underground mirror realm and did not ease until he had finally accepted his love for Loralia and completed his bond with her.

If Lynx had experienced anything like Bannack had when he first met Loralia when he saw Rain, he could only imagine how difficult it was to compound that with not knowing if he would ever see her alive, and then to be infected by the Covra. Being near Rain was the best thing for him as he went through his challenging recovery.

"If the two of you could step back a little," Ciyrs said, holding his hands out to guide Bannack and Pyra back away from Lynx, "I'm going to heal him now."

Bannack and Pyra followed the instruction, taking a few steps back away from Lynx so that Ciyrs could kneel closer to Lynx's prone form. He was not breathing as hard now and his eyes had started to settle, but Bannack knew that wouldn't last. Ciyrs could heal virtually any injury or illness if he got to it fast enough, but the process was neither simple nor pleasant most of the time. The healer pulled Lynx's tattered and bloodied shirt off and tossed it aside before positioning him so that his back was fully accessible.

Ciyrs rubbed his hands together and took a breath before placing them over the gash on Lynx's back. A faint glow appeared under his palms and a moment later Lynx let out a low groan. His body writhed and Bannack could see his hips rise up slightly. It was one of the uncomfortable reactions to the healing process, an unexplained level of arousal that was nearly as sudden and intense as the reaction that came from being close to meeting their mate. This reaction was the primary reason that the warriors preferred to be alone when they were getting healed, and why, even though Ciyrs had been able to transfer some of his impressive healing abilities to his mate when he first healed her, he didn't like it when Elianna healed the men.

After a few minutes of Ciyrs keeping his hands over the gash in Lynx's back, he pulled them away and checked the injury again. Reaching back into his bag, the healer withdrew several bottles and a handful of long bandages. Bannack watched him coat the gash with several thick layers of ointments and ground plants and then look up at Pyra.

"Help me sit him up so that I can bandage him."

Pyra crouched down beside Lynx and propped him up, helping Ciyrs stabilize him as he wrapped the bandages tightly around his body. When he was fully bandaged, the three men lifted Lynx off of the floor and carefully placed him on the bed beside the woman locking in her sleeping state. Though there was enough room on the large bed to place him so that he wasn't touching her, Pyra tucked him under the covers and moved Lynx's hand so that it rested against Rain's arm. Bannack was glad to see this simple gesture. Even though neither of them were conscious, maybe the physical contact would provide some level of comfort and peace.

7

———

Lynx bit down into his bottom lip, withholding a groan as he tried to control himself. He could feel the softness of Rain's mouth making a slow, torturous path down his chest from the soft dip between his collarbones. She followed the touch of her lips with the gentle, almost imperceptible glide of her tongue. When her mouth reached his belly, she let her tongue dip into his navel, and the feeling sent a shiver through his body.

He had never had a craving like he did at that moment, but he didn't want to rush the delicious feelings so he gripped the sheets beside him and squeezed his eyes closed to keep himself from taking her head in his hands and pushing it down.

As if she could sense his need, Rain traced her mouth down the rest of his belly at a slightly faster speed, occasionally following the slick of her tongue with the nip of her teeth against his skin. Finally he could feel her hot, moist breath ripple along the length of his erection and just that one simple sensation caused him to arch his back off of the bed. She waited until he relaxed again to let her tongue trace along him, pausing to concentrate for a few delirious seconds on the sensitive bundle of nerves tucked just under the head before parting her lips further and taking him fully into her mouth.

The feeling nearly overwhelmed him and Lynx continued to struggle to control himself. He wanted to sit up, grab Rain, throw her down, and mate with her until he could no longer move, but at the same time he was reluctant to give up the incredible sensations she was creating inside him and also didn't want to frighten or upset her. It was a delicate balance, at once wanting to take complete control and having enough trust in her to give himself over to her. The combination of the relinquishing control and the hot, intense feeling of her mouth along his cock was something that Lynx had never experienced, but his body moved and reacted on instinct, his hips slowly and subtly rolling to push himself deeper along her tongue to encourage her to suck him harder.

Finally he couldn't control himself anymore and he lifted his hands from the bed, gripping her shoulder with one and burying the other into her hair so that he could guide her into a faster, deeper rhythm. Part of him worried that he had gone too far, that he had exerted too much aggression and dominance over her, but Rain seemed to enjoy it, letting out a soft moan and relaxing her mouth to welcome the thrusts of his hips. As she lowered her body to accept him deeper, Lynx felt her nipples graze against the skin of his thighs and his arousal threatened to topple over.

He pulled her back so that he withdrew from her mouth and took her by her upper arms. Coming up off of the bed, Lynx turned Rain so that he could lower her down onto the bed with her head resting on the pillows where he had just been lying. Her body stretched out beneath him and the impossible, crystal blue of her eyes stared up at him with such openness and trust that he felt his emotions swell almost painfully in his chest. The urgency dissipated as a need to savor and cherish her took over. Lynx lowered his head and touched a kiss to her throat and then another to the soft dip between her collarbones where he could feel her fast heartbeat pounding up at him from beneath her skin.

There was a need for her inside him, something that he could never have explained or even understood before that moment, and he sought to fulfill it completely. His hands stroked down her body, dipping into her curves and memorizing the soft swells of her hips, breasts, and belly. His tongue slid out from between his lips to run a long, slow lick from the valley between her breasts up to the tip of her chin. Her skin tasted warm and salty, her breath rang in his ears, and he could feel her body trembling beneath him. He wanted to experience her with every sense and meld with her into one existence.

Lifting up again to stare into her eyes, Lynx eased himself over her and settled his hips between her thighs. Her long, smooth arms wrapped around his neck and he felt her draw her knees up as if welcoming him into her body. He took a long breath and began to push his hips forward, but just before he sank into her, his eyes snapped open and the entire beautiful image dissolved around him.

Deep, radiating pain in his back overtook the pleasure her mouth had given him, and cold sheets replaced her trembling body. Lynx sat up sharply and gasped at the pain that intensified in his back. His hand came to his chest and he felt the rough bandages. Suddenly things started coming back to him. He remembered the fight with the Covra and the pain of his injuries. He remembered watching Bannack and Pyra fight alongside him. Then he remembered the sudden, all-consuming feeling of hatred and aggression toward the two men. He could feel only the need to destroy them, and then there was blackness.

Lynx dug the heels of his hands into his eyes, rubbing at them to try to clear his mind. He was aware of the feeling of a mattress beneath him and a thick blanket covering from his hips over his legs. His upper body was bare except for the bandages and the cool air of the room sent a chill across his skin. When he pulled his hands away from his eyes he could briefly only see bright colored sparks dancing in the darkness, and then they faded into hazy vision. The room around him was dark, but light from outside came in through the window, allowing him to see what was around him. He glanced down and saw Rain lying beside him, her position unchanged since when he first saw her. Having her so close to him was comforting and he ventured to run his fingers down the curve of her cheek.

As soon as his fingers touched her, Lynx experienced the same sudden flash of vision that he had had the first time he touched her, giving him the same glimpse into the last few seconds of her being awake before the Covra had come out and locked her right there in her bed. Something about the vision struck him strangely this time that hadn't occurred to him the first time. He touched her again, letting himself experience those moments again, and came out of them wondering why she had crawled into bed when the sun was still up and the room was filled with the rich light of late afternoon.

Suddenly he realized that he didn't know where Pyra, Bannack, or any of the other men were. He needed to know what had happened between the moment when he was overcome by the desire to kill them and when he awoke beside Rain. The vivid, intense dream about Rain repeating torturously in his mind, Lynx carefully climbed out of the bed and left the room.

Feeling on edge and worrying that the Covra would suddenly appear again, Lynx took a few steps down the hallway before he heard Pyra's voice from downstairs. He was speaking in a hushed tone, but even speaking as quietly as he could, Pyra wasn't able to keep his voice much lower than what many people would consider a normal conversational tone, and Lynx moved toward it feeling comforted that he didn't feel the compulsion to attack his friend.

"Lynx!" Ciyrs said when Lynx turned the corner from the stairwell into a large open room toward the back of the house.

He didn't remember when the clan's healer had arrived at the house, but he was relieved to see him. He wasn't sure what had happened to him or what exactly Ciyrs had done to ensure that he woke up out of it feeling relatively normal, but he was incredibly relieved that he had been there. From what he could remember feeling in the moments before everything went black, it was very possible that he might not have survived the incident had his friends not acted quickly to ensure that he did.

"It's good to see you up and about, buddy," Pyra said from a couch near a fireplace on the back wall.

"How long have I been out?" Lynx asked, settling gingerly onto another couch beside Bannack.

"A while. Are you feeling alright?" Bannack answered.

"Other than the horrible stabbing pain through my back and being confused as all hell, I think I'm doing fine. Tell me what happened."

As Lynx listened to Pyra and Bannack recount their battle in the bedroom against the Covra and then his sudden descent into a murderous rampage and then Ciyrs's healing, Lynx found his mind continuing to wander back to Rain. He couldn't keep this thoughts off of her, from the look of her lying there locked in her sleep in the bed, to the dream he had had about her as he lay beside her after being healed. As his mind flashed back and forth between the images, something that Pyra said snapped him back into the conversation.

"What?" he asked.

Pyra looked at him quizzically.

"What?"

"What did you just say?"

"I was just saying that you said something about their eyes and then the creatures started leaving, but we didn't know why."

"She didn't see them, so she couldn't fight them," Lynx muttered.

"What are you talking about?" Pyra asked, but Lynx was already on his feet.

"Where are all of the others?"

"They are in the other houses. We decided to stay here for the night before we keep going in the morning so that you could rest."

Lynx was shaking his head and starting for the door before the others could even get up to follow him.

"No. We aren't leaving here until we figure out what's going on, and I think I can help us do that. I need to find Ero."

8

<hr>

Lynx ignored the mutters and the shouted questions when he ran into the main room of the third house down from where he had awoken and rushed directly to Ero where he crouched in front of the fire, prodding at the glowing embers with a sharpened iron rod. The night outside was dramatically colder than the day had been and Lynx could still feel the sting of the air on his skin as he grabbed hold of Ero's back.

"Ero, I need you to come with me."

"Seriously, Lynx? You scared the shit out of me. I could have fallen into the damn fire." He glared at Lynx for a moment before his expression suddenly changed to one of shock, "Lynx! Are you OK? We've all been sitting around scared you weren't going to wake up."

"I'm fine. I need you to do me a favor."

"What do you need?"

"Remember how you were telling me that Zuri sent her journal with you?"

"Yeah, I have it in my bag upstairs."

"Could you get it and come with me?"

Without asking for an explanation, Ero rushed out of the room and Lynx heard his footsteps go up the stairs and down the hall. He could only assume that the house was laid out in essentially the same way as the one where he had been and that Ero was headed to one of the row of bedrooms on the upper floor. A few seconds later he heard the footsteps approaching again and Ero appeared back in the living room gripping the journal and a pencil.

"What do you need me to do?"

A few of the other men in the room had stepped slightly toward him as if waiting for him to include them in what he was saying to Ero, and Lynx turned to them.

"I need everyone to bring their torches and their light sticks. Anything they have that glows."

Lynx waited while the men gathered their light sources from the supplies that they had brought and then led them out onto the street. The warriors who had taken up residence in two other houses along the street came out to meet them, but Lynx told them that they could go back inside and rest. He needed the light, but he didn't need that big of an audience. The men he had already gathered would be enough for what he needed to do.

"What are you doing, Lynx?" Pyra asked as he caught up with Lynx walking toward the front of the compound.

"We need to know what happened to the people here."

"We already know what happened. They got locked by the Covra."

"Right, but there has to be at least one person who fought. One of the Light Ones had to have tried to fight back when they were locking everyone throughout the settlement. We need to find him and see what he did."

"You've lost me."

Lynx stopped in the middle of the road and turned to

look directly into Pyra's face so he could make sure that the larger warrior was listening to him and would follow him.

"I told you that I could see the last few seconds of Rain's life." He felt strangled by the words that he had just said. He didn't want to think that it was true. "The last few seconds before the Covra locked her," he amended, "What if she's not the only one who I can do that with? If there's something about me that lets me see that for all of the locked people, we can piece together exactly what happened."

"It might not work that way," Bannack said.

"Ty can move things with his mind. Ero is impossibly fast. Ciyrs can heal. If they can do those things, why is it so hard to believe that I might have something like that, too? If there is even a chance, we have to try."

"He's right," Pyra said, looking out over the men who had gathered, torches glowing with the flames that they had picked up from the fireplaces and solar-powered light sticks adding their illumination to the pool of light that surrounded them, "This is why we came out here. We want to know what else is out here, and this is part of it. We have to find out what happened."

LYNX LED the men to the front of the settlement, wanting to keep what would likely prove to be a long and exhausting search through every street and building as organized as possible. They gathered at the front gate and he turned to the rest of the men.

"We'll start here and head down the main street first. I'm guessing that's where most of the people will be. We'll work our way down, going into all of the buildings, and then we'll figure out where to go from there."

As one of the youngest and least experienced warriors, it

felt strange to be taking charge in this way, but Lynx knew that he was the only one among them that had the ability to learn what he could about their last moments, and possibly discover how they would be able to reverse the lock and free the entire settlement from the imprisonment they had been suffering unknowingly for so many years.

In the darkness, the unmoving forms of the locked people looked disturbing and Lynx felt himself recoiling from them even as he approached the first person, a man who was frozen mid-step toward the main street. A few of the warriors held up their lights to illuminate the man's face and Lynx could see that his expression didn't seem frightened or anxious, more like he was just walking toward the settlement and was locked without him ever knowing what was happening, just like it was with Rain.

Lynx stepped up to the man cautiously and stared at him for a few seconds, questioning for a moment if he really wanted to do this. It was one thing to look into the last few moments of consciousness for the woman who he knew to be his mate, but this man was a complete stranger, someone who carried no connection for Lynx, and he didn't know if he wanted to go so far as to delve into the privacy of what happened to him right up until he was locked. He knew that he had to do it, though, if the Denynso were ever going to accomplish what they set out to do, and if he was ever going to have a chance to release Rain and be with her in reality.

Apologizing to the unknown man in his mind, Lynx reached out with both hands and rested his palms on the man's arm. Immediately he got the same sensation that he had when he first touched Rain. The world around him seemed to brighten and fade at the same time, and suddenly he was standing not under the cloak of night and the glow of the torches, but in the thick sunlight pouring like amber out of the sky. It was the same late afternoon sunlight he had seen coming through the window of Rain's bedroom in his vision of her last few seconds, and something pulled at his heart as he realized in the seconds that he was experiencing with this man, Rain was down in the main street in her home, brushing through her hair, and readying to climb into bed where she would lie for decades. He wanted so desperately to break away from where he was standing and run down to her house, to fight the Covra that were going to climb out from under her bed, and to protect her from her fate. Something told him, however, that he couldn't do that. He was stuck right there, unable to control himself in the space or anything that was going on around him.

To his side he watched as the man who he had just touched walk from the gate leading into the settlement. He walked calmly with the casual gait of someone who didn't have anything troublesome on his mind. He certainly didn't look like someone who was on guard or worried about an impending battle. The man took several long strides and then Lynx saw one of the Covra scurry through the gate and lash out at the man, digging the end of his sharpened leg into the man's back just as he had done to Rain's stomach. Without even so much as a groan, the man stopped, his foot not quite touching the ground and his eyes still cast down as they opened after blinking. It happened so quickly and then the Covra was gone, rushing down toward the settlement as Lynx saw others starting to climb through windows and across roofs. He couldn't figure out where they were coming from, but they were swarming the settlement at an incredible rate, and none of the Light Ones, the humans whose existence on the planet had either been forgotten or covered up in the generations since this moment, seemed to notice that they were there.

. . .

SEVERAL HOURS later Lynx took a long breath and approached the final person standing on the second street they had explored. Ero stood beside him, the journal in his hands already halfway full of the notes that he wrote down each time that Lynx came out of his vision. They had started the exploration with enthusiasm, talking and sharing ideas as they moved their way along the main street. After more than a dozen people and little information, though, their talk had started to fade. Now Lynx only talked when something extraordinary happened in one of his visions, which meant that for the most part they were walking along in silence.

As he looked at this next person, a woman who seemed locked in the stance of suddenly turning and looking over her shoulder at something, Lynx thought he heard a rustling in one of the buildings to his side. They had just been in that building, however, so he turned back to the woman.

"This has to be it for the night," Pyra said, "We need to sleep. We can keep going as soon as we wake up in the morning."

Lynx gave a defeated sigh and started to lift his hand toward the woman. He heard the rustling sound again and he noticed that the other warriors seemed to be looking around like they heard it, too. It fell silent again and Lynx reached toward the woman. Just as he started to touch her, he could see the first spiked leg of a Covra coming around the edge of the front doorway to the building beside them. Before he could say anything, his palm touched the woman's arm and he disappeared into the vision of her last moments.

The woman was walking away from him and he could see the shadow of a Covra behind her. It was another moment, one like he had had dozens of times since he started looking into these moments, when he wanted so badly to be able to call out to the person, to warn her of what was coming.

Suddenly, almost as if she could hear the screaming in his head, the woman whirled around and confronted the creature. Her eyes flashed as she swung her arm around, bringing a blade up around her and driving it deeply into the eye of the creature. The Covra let out a horrific sound that was between a hiss and a scream, and reared back, pulling its pointed legs up as if ready to strike, and then suddenly collapsing and dissolving into a slick pool of vibrant green blood that seemed to soak down into the ground almost instantly. From one side another of the creatures approached the woman and she shouted. It stumbled back at the sound of her voice and instead of running, she advanced toward it, continuing to yell as she slashed at the creature with her blade. She caught that one in the eye as well, and Lynx watched it recoil and dissolve just as the first.

He was beginning to feel hope when he heard a scratching sound from behind the woman. She turned, glancing over her shoulder, and in an instant before she could even react, a Covra buried its leg into her, locking her in place.

As the vision disappeared around him, Lynx felt himself knocked to the ground. For a moment he had a sense of panic that the Covra had gotten to him again, but he could feel the weight of something massive on top of him and knew that another of the warriors had tackled him to the ground. He heard shouts and felt the weight lifted away from him so that he could roll over and look up to get his bearings about what was happening around him.

The small group of warriors that had come along with him seemed locked in a battle. Three Covra hissed and scurried around them while Ty and an older warrior named Vax growled and rushed toward the other warriors. Lynx knew that they had been infected and that they needed to get rid of the Covra that were there so that they could get these two back to the house for treatment.

"It is their eyes!" Lynx yelled and noticed that the Covra recoiled as if they could understand what he was saying, "Get them in the eyes!"

"Lynx, Bannack, go after the Covra," Pyra commanded, "Ero, Gyyx, Ciyrs, help me."

The warriors split off to follow their orders without question. Out of the corner of his eye Lynx could see Pyra pull off his shirt and the other men follow suit. They tore the garments into long strips and wound them around their hands, tightening the fabric so that it was taut between their grip. Pyra surged forward toward Ty, slamming his shoulder into his belly to flatten him onto the ground. The sudden movement took the infected warrior off guard, causing him to pause for a moment as he tried to catch his breath and get his bearings.

Pyra took advantage of this momentary pause to flip Ty over onto his stomach and use the strips of fabric from his shirt to bind Ty's wrists together. Ero and Gyyx copied his movements on Vax, looping the fabric around his wrists to bind them together and then pulling them back as Pyra did with Ty to attach them to his ankles.

As they did this, Lynx and Bannack advanced toward the Covra. For the first few steps, the creatures seemed to be retreating, then they paused in the still, angry silence of the night air and started rushing toward the two warriors, their hissing sound seeming to rattle through their bodies as they came toward them with their gruesome legs creating deep rivets in the ground and gouges in the side of the building.

Lynx pulled back his blade and brought it over his head with all of the force that he could gather. The Covra in front of him tried to move out of his way, but was blocked by the one standing beside him. The tip of Lynx's blade dug deeply into the creature's eye and he watched it split before the Covra pulled away from him, stumbled back, and dissolved into the ground just as the ones in his vision had. Beside him, Bannack mimicked his action, destroying the Covra in front of him. The final one started scrambling up the wall of the building, and Lynx jumped onto a barrel positioned beside one of the windows and leapt up so that he crossed the path of the Covra, planting a kick in the middle of its body before it could disappear onto the roof. Its body tumbled to the ground beside Bannack, who immediately turned and drove his blade down into the bulbous, gleaming eye.

9
———

"Bannack, you need to slow down."

Loralia held the compact as steady as she could as she rushed across the compound, struggling to decipher the words that Bannack was yelling at her through the glass.

"We figured out that they can only be killed through their eyes," he repeated.

"Their eyes?"

"Yes. Lynx thought that all along, but we spent all night... never mind. I'll explain it all later."

"Are the rest of the men alright?"

"Ciyrs is healing Ty and Vax right now. I think that he got to them in time and that they will be fine. Right now we need to figure out how to get rid of the rest of the Covra. We destroyed those three, but there have to be more. We can't risk them coming out and infecting more of us. If one of them got Ciyrs, there would be nothing that anyone could do."

"Do you know how to lure them to you?" Loralia asked.

"No. They just show up. Do you remember anything else

that your grandfather used to say about the Covra? Anything about when they would come or how you could get them to come out?"

Loralia scoured her mind, trying to recall everything that her grandfather had said, every story that he had told about the creatures and how enemies defeated them. The ground pounded beneath her feet as she ran toward the forest.

"Silence," she said, suddenly remembering one of the stories as she dropped down onto the ground and moved aside a section of moss to reveal the hole leading down into her mirror realm.

"Silence?" Bannack asked.

"Yes. One of the stories that my grandfather used to tell was about how the greatest enemies of the Covra had a power that would weaken the creatures and was the only thing that could reverse their greatest defense, and that silence was their comfort and their joy."

"What was the greatest defense?"

"He never said."

Bannack didn't respond and Loralia dropped down through the hole into the home that she had had her entire life before she met Bannack and agreed to go above ground to be his mate.

"Locking them," Bannack said a moment later, sounding as if he was speaking more to himself than to her.

"Locking?" she asked.

Loralia listened while Bannack told him about the warriors visiting the prison that they had thought belonged to the Klimnu but they discovered actually belonged to the Covra, and how they found out about the kingdom that the Covra had locked. He detailed the Light Ones and how they appeared to be frozen in place in the same breath that they had been drawing when the Covra attacked them. As she listened, Loralia tried to understand what he was telling her, and what she might be able to do to help him. She had gone to the mirror realm to surround herself in what was familiar, hoping that it would help her to think clearly. She could feel that her mate was frightened and upset, and she wanted to do anything that she could to help him.

She moved deeper into the caverns, exploring the chambers and venturing into areas that she hadn't visited in quite some time. Suddenly she saw something that made her heart pound faster and a smile come to her lips for the first time since the day that Bannack left.

"Do you remember what I told you about the compact?" she asked, looking into the mirror at him.

Bannack nodded.

"Whatever reflects in your mirror, reflects in mine."

"Yes. And do you remember what happens when something reflects in my bottom mirror from the top?"

"It becomes real."

Loralia nodded and looked back across the cavern.

BANNACK CROUCHED DOWN behind the barrel he had pulled into the middle of the street and glanced over at Lynx who sat beside him. The others had remained in the buildings on either side of the street, poised beside the windows and doors to watch what was happening, but staying out of sight.

"Are you sure that this is going to work?" Lynx whispered.

"It has to," Bannack answered. "In order for it to, though, you have to believe that it will. Loralia can only make this happen if you completely believe that it is going to work the way that she intends it to. If you don't, it won't exist, do you understand?" Lynx nodded and Bannack nodded back at him, "Good. Now we have to be completely silent."

The two warriors fell silent and Bannack glanced down at the compact in his hand. Loralia's face gazed up at him from the glass, her beautiful lavender eyes calm and focused. Nervousness flooded through Bannack, but he knew that he had to steady himself so that he could do his part of Loralia's plan properly. After several minutes of waiting, he heard the rustling sound that told him the Covra were approaching. The sound seemed louder and deeper than it had before and Bannack knew that meant there were more of the creatures this time as if they had sent more to seek revenge on those who had destroyed three of their number just hours before.

"They're coming," Bannack mouthed to Loralia, not making a sound.

Loralia nodded. Bannack lifted up slightly so that he could look over the barrel and watch the Covra approaching.

"Patient," Loralia mouthed to him.

Bannack watched until they were close enough that they would be able to see him clearly and then stood, pulling Lynx up with him so that they were standing in the middle of the street, open to the swarm of creatures approaching. He could feel Lynx tense beside him, but Bannack stood steady. Lynx adjusted his grip on the blade beside him. It was meant as both a ruse and a backup plan just in case Loralia's idea fell through. They waited for a few more tense seconds, the time seeming to drag past as they allowed the creatures to get dangerously closer. Bannack's heart pounded in his chest and his head felt like it was swimming. If this didn't work, the entirety of the group could be killed, many by each other's hands.

In an instant, the plan mobilized around him. The Covra climbing along the outside walls of the buildings got close to the windows and doors, and the warriors inside started to shout. As they yelled, the creatures paused and started to retreat from the sound. They started moving backwards back down the street, but several of the warriors streamed out of the building and made a line across the street, blocking them with a wall of sound. The creatures turned and started scurrying more quickly toward Bannack and Lynx, unable to go anywhere else.

"Are you ready?" Bannack asked, looking down at Loralia.

"Just hold your compact so that the bottom mirror is straight upright and the top mirror is tilted toward it. Go!"

Bannack turned the compact in his hand and held it as Loralia instructed. There was a moment when nothing happened and he felt his stomach turn, but he closed his eyes and forced himself to believe with every bit of his existence that she would create exactly what she intended to. His eyes still closed, Bannack suddenly heard the hissing, screeching sound of the Covra dying. He opened his eyes and found himself staring at a massive slab of brown and grey rock.

After several long seconds the screaming stopped and a chilling quiet settled over the street. Finally it broke with the sound of Loralia laughing.

"We might not be able to communicate with our thoughts, my love, but how many of the other warriors can do that?"

Bannack could hear the other warriors cheering and shouting, but it took a few moments before he was able to get his thoughts together enough to walk around the stone slab toward the cheering. When he did he saw the green blood of the Covra soaking into the dirt of the road, dripping from the rock spikes protruding from the front of the slab.

"What is that?" he asked.

"The floor of one of the caverns," Loralia told him, "I used to play on them when I was younger. I remembered how sharp they were."

"You are incredible."

"No, darling, you are."

"What, now? Is this thing just going to stay here?"

"If you think that it is part of settlement now, then it is. If not, when you close the compact, it will disappear."

"Then it will stay, forever a reminder of what destroyed the Covra."

Suddenly Loralia's eyes grew dark.

"This isn't the end, Bannack," she said solemnly.

The words hit him and the sound of the celebrating warriors seemed to fade.

"What do you mean?"

"I can still feel them. They're angry, Bannack. There's more to come. You need to save the Light Ones or very soon they will be lost forever."

TBC

(To be continued in Part V...)